This Ladybird Book belongs to:

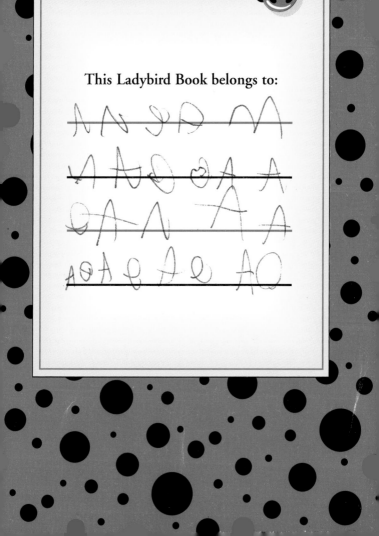

retold by Nicola Baxter
illustrated by Tony Kenyon

Cover illustration by John Gurney

Originally published in the United Kingdom by Ladybird Books Ltd © 1993

First American edition by Ladybird Books USA
An Imprint of Penguin USA Inc.
375 Hudson Street, New York, New York 10014

Printed in Great Britain
10 9 8 7 6 5 4 3 2 1

ISBN 0-7214-5647-2

FAVORITE TALES

Puss in
Boots

nce upon a time, there was a miller who had three sons. When the miller died, he left the mill to his eldest son and a donkey to his second son. Soon each was able to earn a good living.

But all that the youngest son got was his father's cat.

"Poor Puss," said the miller's son. "What shall we do?"

"Don't worry," said the cat. "Give me a pair of boots and a bag, and we will do very well together."

When the miller's son brought the things the cat wanted, Puss got to work. He pulled on his boots, filled the bag with lettuce leaves, and put it in a field.

Very soon, a little rabbit came to nibble the lettuce.

Quick as a flash, Puss caught the rabbit in his bag. Then he carried it to the King's palace.

"Your Majesty," said Puss, "please accept this fine rabbit as a present from my master, the Marquis of Carrabas."

"I've never heard of him," said the King, "but you deserve a treat from the kitchen."

The next day, Puss learned that the King and his daughter would be driving by the river.

"Master," he said, "do what I say, and we shall be rich. You must take off your clothes and swim in the river. And you must pretend that your name is the Marquis of Carrabas."

"I've never heard of him," said the miller's son, "but I'll do as you say, Puss."

Before long, the King drove up with his daughter, the Princess. He was pleased to see Puss again.

"Your Majesty," said Puss, bowing low, "a terrible thing has happened! While my master, the Marquis of Carrabas, was swimming in the river, some thieves came along and stole all of his clothes!"

"How dreadful!" exclaimed the King and the Princess together.

At once, the King sent to the palace for
some clothes. When the miller's son put
them on, he looked very handsome.

"Please come and ride in my carriage,"
said the King. "And I shall introduce
you to my daughter."

Puss quickly ran ahead to a field where some farmers were cutting hay. "The King is coming," he shouted to them. "If he asks, you must say that this land belongs to the Marquis of Carrabas."

"We've never heard of him," said the farmers, "but we'll do as you say."

Soon the King drove up in his carriage with the Princess and the miller's son. "Tell me, my man," said the King, "whose land is this?"

"It belongs to the Marquis of Carrabas, Your Majesty," the man replied politely.

Meanwhile, Puss had discovered that the land really belonged to an ogre who lived in a huge castle nearby.

Puss quickly made his way to the castle and knocked on the door. "Sir, is it true that you are an excellent magician?" he asked the ogre.

The ogre, who liked to show off, replied, "Of course it's true. I can even turn myself into a lion!"

In an instant, the ogre became a fierce, roaring lion!

Puss was so startled that he scrambled to
the top of a chest of drawers to hide.

When the ogre had changed himself back again, Puss jumped down. "Turning into a lion must be easy for someone as big and strong as you," he said. "But can you turn yourself into something tiny—like a mouse?"

"Of course I can!" roared the ogre. "Just watch!"

In the blink of an eye, the ogre became
a little mouse scurrying across the floor.
Puss instantly pounced on
him and ate him up.

"Now that the ogre is gone," Puss said to
himself, "this castle will make a very fine
home for my master, the Marquis of
Carrabas."

The King was impressed by the handsome young man who owned such rich land and lived in such a magnificent castle. "He will make a fine husband for my daughter," the King said.

So the miller's son, the Princess, and Puss lived happily ever after. And now everyone has heard of the Marquis of Carrabas!

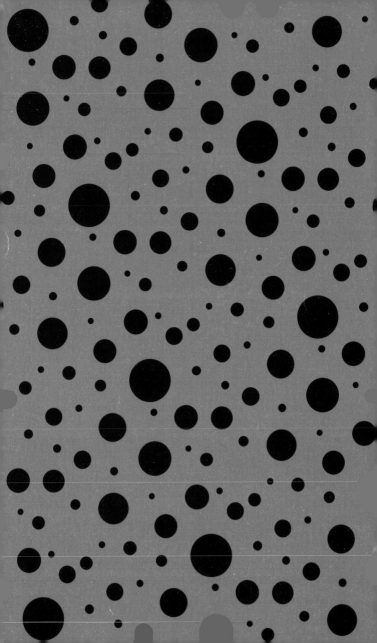